LEGO

THE LEGO MOVIE

KEEPING IT AWESOMER WITH EMMET

SCHOLASTIC INC.

ISBN: 978-1-338-30758-0

10 9 8 7 6 5 4 3 2 1   19 20 21 22 23

Printed in China   95
First printing 2019

Book design by Marissa Asuncion

TABLE OF CONTENTS

EVERYTHING IS AWESOME . . . ?

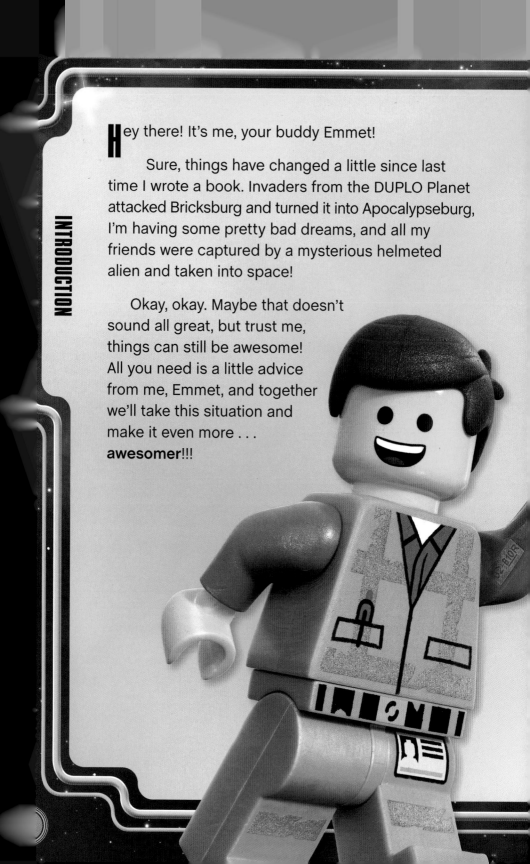

Hey there! It's me, your buddy Emmet!

Sure, things have changed a little since last time I wrote a book. Invaders from the DUPLO Planet attacked Bricksburg and turned it into Apocalypseburg, I'm having some pretty bad dreams, and all my friends were captured by a mysterious helmeted alien and taken into space!

Okay, okay. Maybe that doesn't sound all great, but trust me, things can still be awesome! All you need is a little advice from me, Emmet, and together we'll take this situation and make it even more . . . **awesomer**!!!

When things seem dark and gloomy, just think, "I'll make it better!"

First, I guess I should explain how Apocalypseburg came to be. You see, after Taco Tuesday, things seemed pretty awesome in Bricksburg. The city was saved. Lord Business wasn't trying to glue the world together anymore. And my friends and I were all ready to party!

Everything was awesome, and then . . . a bunch of alien invaders from the DUPLO Planet showed up at the exact moment we thought we were safe, and wanted to destroy us. I tried to say we were friendly by building them a big Welcome Heart, but instead of hugging and squeezing the Welcome Heart, they kind of . . . ate it. Then the aliens started eating *all* the bricks in Bricksburg.

We tried to fight back, but the aliens just kept coming. Before we knew it, Bricksburg was in ruins. Apocalypseburg was born!

THE TRANSFORMATION OF BRICKSBURG TO APOCALYPSEBURG

1: First it was party time!

2: Then these guys crashed the party.

3: Then they ATE the party!

4: Now there ain't no party.

NEW AND IMPROVED BEST FRIENDS

What do you do when the apocalypse comes? You get an upgrade, of course! My best buddies, the Master Builders, got ultra-cool, end-of-the-world upgrades to help them stay awesome during the apocalypse.

LUCY

Lucy took a hardened-heart approach to things. When she's not kicking DUPLO alien butt, she relaxes by having brooding sessions overlooking the Apocalypseburg wasteland. Just look at how brooding she is!

ULTRAKATTY

Unikitty accessed her inner rage and now she's Ultrakatty. Ultrakatty has claws EVERYWHERE. On a scale of one to ten, she's taken this whole claw thing to 107.

BATMAN

I didn't know that Batman could look any more hardcore. But then, he *did*. Suped-up chest plate. Black-on-darker-black camo. The apocalypse looks good on him, don't you think?

METALBEARD

Metalbeard uses leftover scraps that he finds to enhance his armor. Rebuilding his body from scratch is actually kind of routine for him at this point.

BENNY

And then there's my good friend Benny. He's still really into spaceships. Now he has a robotic arm to build them.

NEW AND IMPROVED ENEMIES

Just when my friends and I got into the groove of the apocalypse lifestyle, I had a dream. Well, not really a dream—a scary dream. Lucy was taken by aliens and taken to a secret ceremony that was at 5:15 p.m. I guess you could say I was relieved when I woke up and Lucy *hadn't* been abducted by aliens!

But then . . . a new batch of aliens came, and they were even stranger than the DUPLO ones! They had heart weapons and really impressive armor! They took my friends, including Lucy . . . and guess where they were taking them?! A secret ceremony at 5:15 p.m.!!! Talk about weird, right?

I'm not entirely clear what the ceremony is supposed to be but that's not the point. The point is, these guys forced me to get tough and set out on an entirely new adventure to rescue all the people I care about! You might call it the second part of my new adventure. Life's funny like that sometimes.

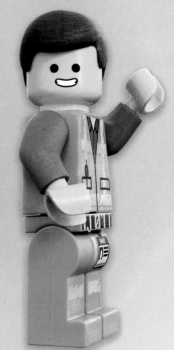

SWEET MAYHEM

I have a real brick to pick with this alien commander. She swooped in on her awesome-looking spaceship, pumped out some sweet techno beats, and then captured my friends using exploding smiley-face hearts and a sticker gun. A STICKER gun! If I weren't so steamed at her for threatening everything and everyone I love, I'd probably want her autograph.

QUEEN WATEVRA WA'NABI

Queen Watevra Wa'nabi sounds kinda awesome when you say it out loud, right? Queen Watevra Wa'nabi! I almost want to shout it! Anyway, Sweet Mayhem took my friends to a place called the Systar System ruled by—deep breath—Queen Watevra Wa'nabi. Not gonna lie, I do not know what to make of this alien queen. She can shape-shift, which means she can take the shape of a dolphin or of a blobby, amorphous thing. Oh, and she sings. *A lot.*

BALTHAZAR

Balthazar is a teenage vampire who oversees the Shambhala Health Spa and Mindfulness Center on Queen Watevra Wa'nabi's Planet of Infinite Reflection. Why would a bunch of aliens run a health spa on a remote planet, you ask? No idea.

BUNNY MASSEUSE

This bunny masseuse uses hot stones to brainwash—I mean, massage you—at the Shambhala Health Spa and Mindfulness Center.

ICE CREAM CONE

And Queen Watevra Wa'nabi's
right-hand henchman is an . . .
ice cream cone. I guess that's cool?
Or cold, depending on how literally
you're taking things.

REX DANGERVEST
MY VEST FRIEND!

Now this guy—THIS GUY—is *awesome*.
Unlike those wacky new folks, Rex
Dangervest is my vest friend. (Get it?
Vest friend? Because we both wear vests?)
He's a galaxy-jumping, raptor-training,
archaeologist cowboy who likes building
furniture and having an effortlessly natural smile
in photographs. Don't tell Batman, but Rex may
just be the coolest guy who's ever saved my life.

GET READY TO GET AWESOME (AGAIN!)

Now it's time to tap into our inner awesome as we face the unknown—together! That's better than doing it alone, right?

IT'S TIME TO HUTT-HUTT, KICK SOME BUTT!

EMMET

EMMET'S GUIDE TO SURVIVING APOCALYPSEBURG

WELCOME TO APOCALYPSEBURG

Apocalypseburg might sound scary, but it's not so bad—the trick is to see the beauty through the dust. (And destruction. And general wasteland.) Here are some of my favorite things to keep in mind when waking up to another hot, haze-filled morning in Apocalypseburg.

EMMET'S TIPS FOR APPRECIATING THE APOCALYPSE

1. Things are constantly getting destroyed, which means there's always room for reconstruction. That's great for a construction worker like me!

2. Black and brown camo is a very flattering color scheme.

3. We still have an overpriced coffee shop. And who doesn't love over-priced coffee? Nobody! Score!

4. Because civilization has moved underground to survive the toxic-waste zones, we now have . . . sewer babies! So cute!

BATTENING DOWN THE HATCHES

We learned about the importance of a rock-solid sanctuary pretty quick after the DUPLO aliens attacked! Thankfully, there was one expert on secret fortified hideouts—and that someone was . . .

THAT'S RIGHT. ME. BATMAN. YOU'RE WELCOME.

BATMAN'S CITADEL

What's in Batman's Citadel? Well, for starters, there are thirty-foot-high, three-foot-thick stone walls. Legions of battle vehicles parked and at the ready. Torch-flame lights, massive steel doors that close very slowly, and a butler named Alfred to man them. Suffice it to say, Batman's Citadel is the most kick-butt place to wait out an alien raid.

QUALITY TIME WITH FRIENDS

Naturally, all that time spent in close quarters meant we had plenty of opportunities to bond with one another. And trust me, you haven't really bonded with someone until you've hunkered down with them for a week-long barrage of extraterrestrial missiles and endured an accidental sewage leak into the water system that left you without coffee for **seven whole days**!!!

I ADMIRE YOUR RESTRAINT UNDER PRESSURE. YOU'RE PURRING!

I'M NOT PURRING. I'M RUMBLING WITH RAGE.

MAKING LEMONADE OUT OF DUST AND ASHES

Of course, mega-reinforced shelters aren't the only things that are important to create during the end of the world. Sometimes the best way to push down the bleak thoughts is to build something with your best buddies just for funsies. Sure, there's a 99.999999% chance what you build will get destroyed. But there's a 0.000001% chance it might *not*.

HOME SWEET HOME

Lucy always seemed so sad thinking about the way Bricksburg used to be. I wanted her to be happy again. So I surprised her with an awesome house constructed in the middle of the wasteland! What it lacked in iron bars and security systems, it made up for in style. Plus, it was the first one on the cul-de-sac. Getting in early on that housing market never felt so good!

EMMET'S AWESOME HOUSE CHECKLIST

• LIVING ROOM (where we'll live it up)	☐
• TELEVISION ROOM (where we'll watch it up)	☐
• BREAKFAST NOOK (where we'll eat it up)	☐
• MEDITATION ROOM (where we'll—I mean, I'll—meditate it up)	☐
• BROODING ROOM (where Lucy'll brood it up)	☐
• KITTY CAT ROOM (where cats will cat it up)	☐
• FIREMAN'S POLE (where we will slide it up—or down)	☐
• WATERSLIDE SYSTEM (where we'll WATERSLIDE it up, down, and spin it all around)	☐
• TRAMPOLINE COMPLEX (where we'll jump it up)	☐
• TOASTER ROOM (where we'll waffle it up, any time of day)	☐

DARK AND BROODING PHRASE CONVERTER

A lot of Apocalypseburgers like to vent their deeper thoughts in a dark and brooding way. Not speaking the lingo can lead to confusing miscommunication. So I came up with this handy-dandy converter chart to help understand what they're saying. Take a look!

WHAT AN APOCALYPSEBURGER SAYS:	WHAT IT MEANS:
"We've awoken to another day of destruction and despair."	"Good morning!"
"I see the devastation hasn't yet crushed your soul."	"You look nice."
"Come. Let us seek the bitter liquid that provides the only semblance of pleasure left in these dark times."	"Let's grab a coffee."
"The clouds formed from our evaporated tears have parted, revealing a raging orb of flame."	"It's sunny out."
"Battle hardens the heart."	"When the going gets tough, the tough get going."
Solemn, silent nod	"Hi!"

What would your favorite phrase sound like if it was all dark and brooding?

EMMET'S DOS AND DON'TS
OF APOCALYPSEBURG

As Lucy likes to say, a jaunt through Apocalypseburg isn't for the faint of heart. But if you keep these easy "dos" and "don'ts" in mind, you'll be right on track to toughing it out! (Or at least giving the impression that you've cultivated a totally hard-edged side that's super tough.)

DO: Watch where you're walking. You never know when a caravan of cyborgs is going to emerge from the manhole you're standing on.

DO: Get to the Coffee Unchained shop early. There's always a long line.

DON'T: Cut the line at Coffee Unchained. People in Apocalypseburg take their coffee super seriously. I'm pretty sure a few battles blamed on the alien invaders may have actually been over coffee.

DO: Map out the fastest route to Batman's Citadel from any given point in da 'burg. You do *not* want to be that guy stranded outside when the steel doors shut.

DON'T: Ask Surfer Dave for a surfing lesson. He goes by Chainsaw Dave now and all his surfboards are kind of cut in half and don't float very well.

DO: Remember to pet Sherry's cats: Scarfield, Deathface, Metalscratch, Razor, Laserbeam, Fingernail, and Tox and Toes. They get whiny when they don't get TLC.

DO NOT: PET SHERRY'S CAT, JEFF. That cat still has major 'tude.

DO: Spend time with your friends, even if it's playing a game of Dustbowl Ball, or my personal favorite, Sewer Jump.

DO: Try to see the bright side in everything. Because if you can't smile at the funny little moments in life that something small and silly like an apocalypse brings, then what's the point?

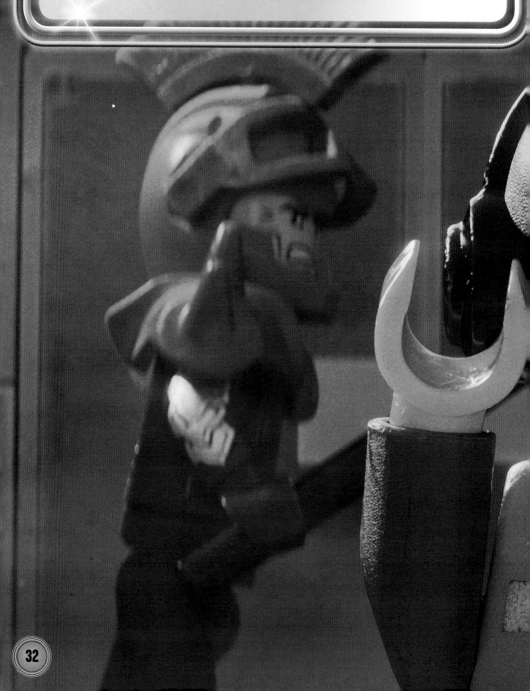

EMMET'S AWESOME PIECE OF ADVICE #1: IT'S ALL ABOUT SEEING THE BRIGHT SIDE.

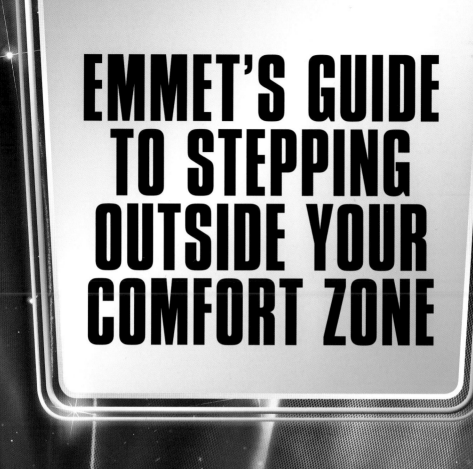

EMMET'S GUIDE TO STEPPING OUTSIDE YOUR COMFORT ZONE

WHEN TROUBLE COMES KNOCKING

When Sweet Mayhem busted into Batman's Citadel and announced that five of our fiercest leaders were invited to a "Ceremonial Ceremony at 5:15 p.m." in the unknown Systar System, we had no idea what she was talking about. But she wasn't exactly the sit-down-and-explain-it-over-a-cup-of-tea-and-a-delicious-scone type (wouldn't that have been great if she was?). Instead of treating us to a scone, she captured Lucy, Batman, Ultrakatty, Metalbeard, and Benny and zoomed off! Talk about a buzzkill!

INTO THE UNKNOWN

I couldn't believe it. All of my best friends were in trouble. Someone had to save them! But it would mean traveling past the dreaded Stairgate and into the Systar System. The Justice League had tried to make it past the Stairgate years ago and were never heard from again. And with Batman gone, there were no Super Heroes left.

There was only one thing to do: I would have to leave the only world I'd ever known and journey into uncharted territory, solo.

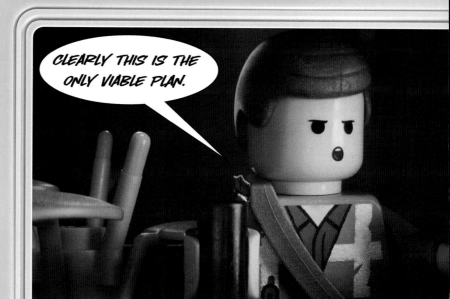

CLEARLY THIS IS THE ONLY VIABLE PLAN.

ADORABLE
HOUSE ROCKET
FOR THE WIN!

BEYOND THE STAIRGATE

Sure, no one had ever made it past the Stairgate and lived to tell the tale. But I was ready. I was PUMPED! And . . . I was almost immediately pulverized by an asteroid. Man, people weren't kidding when they said the Stairgate was deadly. It's DEADLY!

Luckily for me, a renegade rebel named Rex Dangervest flew in from out of nowhere and saved my butt. I'm not sure what would have happened if Rex hadn't shown up. I probably would have ended up lost and forgotten in some abandoned corner of the universe. Phew—close call.

> ### STEPPING OUTSIDE YOUR COMFORT ZONE LESSON #1:
> It helps to have someone with you who knows what they're doing.

MIND IF I SAVE YOUR LIFE? RAD.

REXCELSIOR

Rex drives a hardcore spaceship called the Rexcelsior. I thought my house rocket was cool, but this bad boy boasts a hyper-lightspeed combustor, warp-drive system that cranks to eleven (times two!), and even a self-destruct button. Can't go on any intergalactic space mission without one of those.

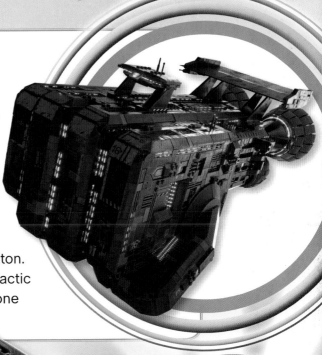

MEGA-AWESOME SPACESHIP FOR THE EVEN BETTER WIN!

RAPTORS

Oh yeah. Rex has raptors too. More on these guys later.

ENTER THE SYSTAR SYSTEM

Once Rex and I got past the Stairgate, things got even weirder. The Systar System is made up of a bunch of crazy, laws-of-physics-breaking worlds that we would have to explore in order to find where Sweet Mayhem had taken my friends.

PLANTIMAL PLANET

This Plantimal planet may look pretty and sparkly, but BEWARE. The cute little Plantimal inhabitants are savage. They eat everything in sight. I think they may have eaten some of Rex's raptors . . .

HARMONY TOWN (AKA HECK)

The people here are all perfect. Too perfect. They like to surround you and sing hypnotic songs that get stuck in your head until you feel like you're just as perfect as them and everything around you is perfect and sparkly and . . . wow. Just thinking about it gets to me.

PLANET OF INFINITE REFLECTION

The Planet of Infinite Reflection is home to the Shambhala Health Spa and Mindfulness Center. This is where Sweet Mayhem took my friends to trick them into feeling super cheerful and not at all suspicious of Queen Watevra Wa'nabi.

STEPPING OUTSIDE YOUR COMFORT ZONE LESSON #2:

Be open to new experiences. But also be ready to run. Or else you might get eaten. Or brainwashed. Or both.

DECIPHERING WEIRD VISIONS OF THE FUTURE

Remember that dream I mentioned before? I mean, that nightmare? Well, let me tell you allllll about it.

In it there was a dolphin wearing a top hat—I think it was a dolphin, anyway. It might have been a whale or a shark or a narwhal, but it was *definitely* shaped like a marine animal of some kind. And on its chest was a clock that said 5:15 p.m. At that moment, everyone I ever cared about was sucked up into a giant black void in space. It was Armageddon—the actual end times. Nothing. Zilch. Nada.

That's why I had to find my friends and stop whatever ceremony was taking place at 5:15 p.m. If I didn't, everything would be . . . gone.

STEPPING OUTSIDE YOUR COMFORT ZONE LESSON #3:
If you have a weird dream about a dolphin with a clock on its chest, it's probably a vision of the future.

When have you stepped outside your comfort zone to help the people you love?

EMMET'S TOP FIVE TIPS FOR TRAVELING OUTSIDE YOUR COMFORT ZONE

Don't worry if you're more of a homebody than a travel buddy. I've taken the guesswork out of traversing into the unknown for you. Here are the best tips I learned along the way:

TOP FIVE TIPS

1. PACK FOR ALL KINDS OF WEATHER. THIS IS THE TIME TO BUST OUT YOUR GRANDMA'S HOMESPUN TURTLENECK!

2. MAKE SURE YOU HAVE A TRAVEL PLAN. AS IN, HOW QUICKLY CAN YOU TURN AROUND AND HEAD HOME IF THINGS ARE TOO OVERWHELMING?

3. IT HELPS TO HAVE A GUIDE. SOMEONE WHO'S GOT YOUR BACK AND WILL HELP YOU *NOT* DIE. USUALLY I'D RECOMMEND BATMAN FOR THIS, BUT I GUESS THAT'S *NOT* REALLY HELPFUL IF BATMAN'S MIA.

4. MY BIGGEST TIP? CATCH A RIDE WITH SOMEONE WHO OWNS A DELUXE SPACESHIP EXPONENTIALLY MORE POWERFUL THAN YOUR OWN! IT'LL REALLY HELP YOU OUT!

5. IN GENERAL, YOUR BEST BET FOR LEAVING YOUR COMFORT ZONE *IS* TO FIND SOMEONE WHO IS COMFORTABLE IN THAT ZONE AND TAKE THEM WITH YOU.

COMFORT IS OVERRATED.

EMMET'S AWESOME PIECE OF ADVICE #2: NEVER SAY "NO" WHEN SOMEONE OFFERS TO SAVE YOUR LIFE.

EMMET'S GUIDE TO AMPING UP YOUR "LET'S STOP ARMAGEDDON" STYLE

Now that you know how to survive and navigate the apocalypse, it's time to make sure you look good while doing it.

Style makeovers always give me an instant pick-me-up!

APOCALYPSEBURG STYLE

DON'T-MESS-WITH-ME FACEMASK
Make sure to pair it with your sickest mohawk.

INFRARED GOGGLES
Chic *and* functional.

WELDER'S MASK AND SPEAR
Nothing says "I'm a hard worker and I'm not ashamed to show it" like combining elements from your work and play wardrobe together.

EYE PATCH
The *it* accessory of the year.

AMPED-UP SUPER HERO STYLE

If you're going to be a Super Hero during the apocalypse, your style needs to be functional *and* inspirational. Remember: The masses are looking up to you!

BEEFED-UP BATMAN

When Batman heard it was the apocalypse, he basically said "challenge accepted." Now he's darker and brooding-er than before. His Batarangs are even blacker. Because apocalypse.

CYBER-ARM AND SPIKED-FLAIL BENNY

Benny carries around two spiked flails that somehow will help him build spaceships. It's all a little fuzzy. But he says it makes sense.

MOTORBIKE METALBEARD

Metalbeard put his pedal to the metal and built a tripped-out pirate motorbike. It has spiked hubcaps, razor-blade wheels, double-blaster cannons, and his trademark shark missile. And a wooden steering wheel. He tells me that's called *panache*.

FIERY-CLAWED ULTRAKATTY

Ultrakatty has taken this whole apocalypse thing a little personally and fueled her style with pure rage. You know how she used to be super sweet and positive all the time? Now she's, like, not.

RENEGADE LOOKS FOR TRAVELING INTO THE UNKNOWN

And then there are the looks that are just the *coolest*. Everything about Rex Dangervest is kick-butt personified. Even his name drips style. *Dangervest*! I couldn't have come up with a better cool-guy name myself if I tried! Also, he may just have the best vest in the known universe, and I think even Batman would agree.

THE ANATOMY OF A LONE-WOLF WARDROBE

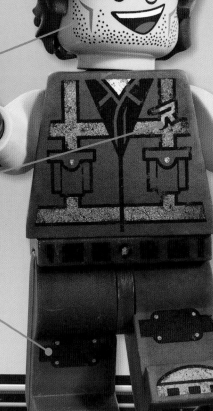

STUBBLE
(ALWAYS A
RUGGED CHOICE)

SWEET VEST WITH PERSONALLY
COMMISSIONED LOGO

CHAPS
(THEY'RE BASICALLY
LEG VESTS)

RAPTORS

Rex Dangervest's best buddies are *raptors*. Repeat that back—raptors. Who can skateboard. And jet-pack. And pilot his spaceship. I don't . . . I can't . . . I did not know that much cool could reside in one individual, but I'll say it one more time to let that sink in. Raptors.

NATURALLY FLOWING HAIR WITH AN "I DON'T CARE" GALACTIC-SURFER VIBE

COLOR-COORDINATED WORK GLOVES (BUT WE ALL KNOW THEY'RE JUST FOR SHOW. THIS ROCK STAR ISN'T AFRAID TO GET HIS HANDS DIRTY.)

TAPPING INTO YOUR SUPED-UP STYLE

As for me, my wardrobe hasn't changed much since Taco Tuesday. I still like orange. Oh! Well, I *did* laminate my name tag so I wouldn't have to keep replacing it when it got scorched by alien laser beams. So there's that.

You know what's even more important than outward apparel, though? Inner style! Seriously!

When my friends got kidnapped, I broke out my most gosh-darned determined furrowed brow and "let's do this" stare. Because when you're determined, anything is possible. And it's awesome!!!

Want to try having a new inner style at home? You can practice this in the mirror if you want! (Or something reflective, like maybe Batman's shiny black armor—if you manage to get close enough, that is.) Look at your reflection and make a nice, determined face. But not so determined that you look like you're having a bad day on the toilet. You'll want to look like your eye is on the prize. And cool, calm, and collected. Just like me. I'm the most cool, calm, and collected person I know!

WHAT WOULD YOUR INTERGALACTIC "LET'S STOP ARMAGEDDON" STYLE LOOK LIKE?

Are you the type to hunker down and guard the roost during the end times? Or are you the planet-hopping rogue who throws caution to the space wind (vacuum?) and brings extinct animals along for the ride? Choose one item from each of the columns below to discover your "Let's Stop Armageddon" style.

OUTERWEAR	LEGWEAR	HEADWEAR	ACCESSORIES
Vests	Steel-toed boots	Space helmet	Eye patch
Flame-resistant stealth suit	Utility pants with LOTS of pockets	Iron muzzle	Exploding smiley-face hearts and stars
Very practical construction jacket	Rocket boosters	Welder's mask	Raptors
Chain mail	Chaps	Flowing locks of well-conditioned hair	Surprisingly green and vibrant Planty
Jet-pack space suit	Stretchy pants	Knit cap	Scarf

**EMMET'S AWESOME PIECE OF ADVICE #3:
ALWAYS PLACE YOUR UNCONDITIONAL
TRUST IN LIFESAVING HEROES.
LIKE BATMAN.**

EMMET'S GUIDE TO BEING TOUGH

TOUGH IT UP

If there's one thing I've learned from this post-apocalyptic, intergalactic space journey, it's that when the going gets tough, you have to get tougher. And no one is better at dialing up the toughness than my best buddies. Check out the cool tips I've learned from them about channeling your inner hardcore.

ULTRAKATTY, WE'RE GOING ON A RECON MISSION, STAT.

LUCY'S TIPS FOR BEING TOUGH

- BATTLE HARDENS US ALL.

- NEVER STOP FIGHTING.

- DON'T LOOK BACK. I DON'T EVEN LIKE TO LOOK IN THE REARVIEW MIRROR.

- BROODING SESSIONS ARE A GET-TOUGH MUST.

- HAVE A BIG HEART.

EMMET'S FIRST ATTEMPT TO GET TOUGH

Lucy's a great teacher, but I'm always so excited to see her, it's tricky learning to brood.

REMEMBER EMMET, LOOK TO THE FUTURE. NEVER LOOK BACK.

I ALWAYS LOOK FORWARD. SOMETIMES WHILE ADMIRING ENHANCED BINOCULARS.

YOU GOT IT, LUCY! I PROMISE I'M GOING TO CULTIVATE A TOTALLY HARD-EDGED SIDE THAT'S SUPER TOUGH AND—

OH! OH! LOOK—A SHOOTING STAR! MAKE A WISH!

TOUGH FAIL!

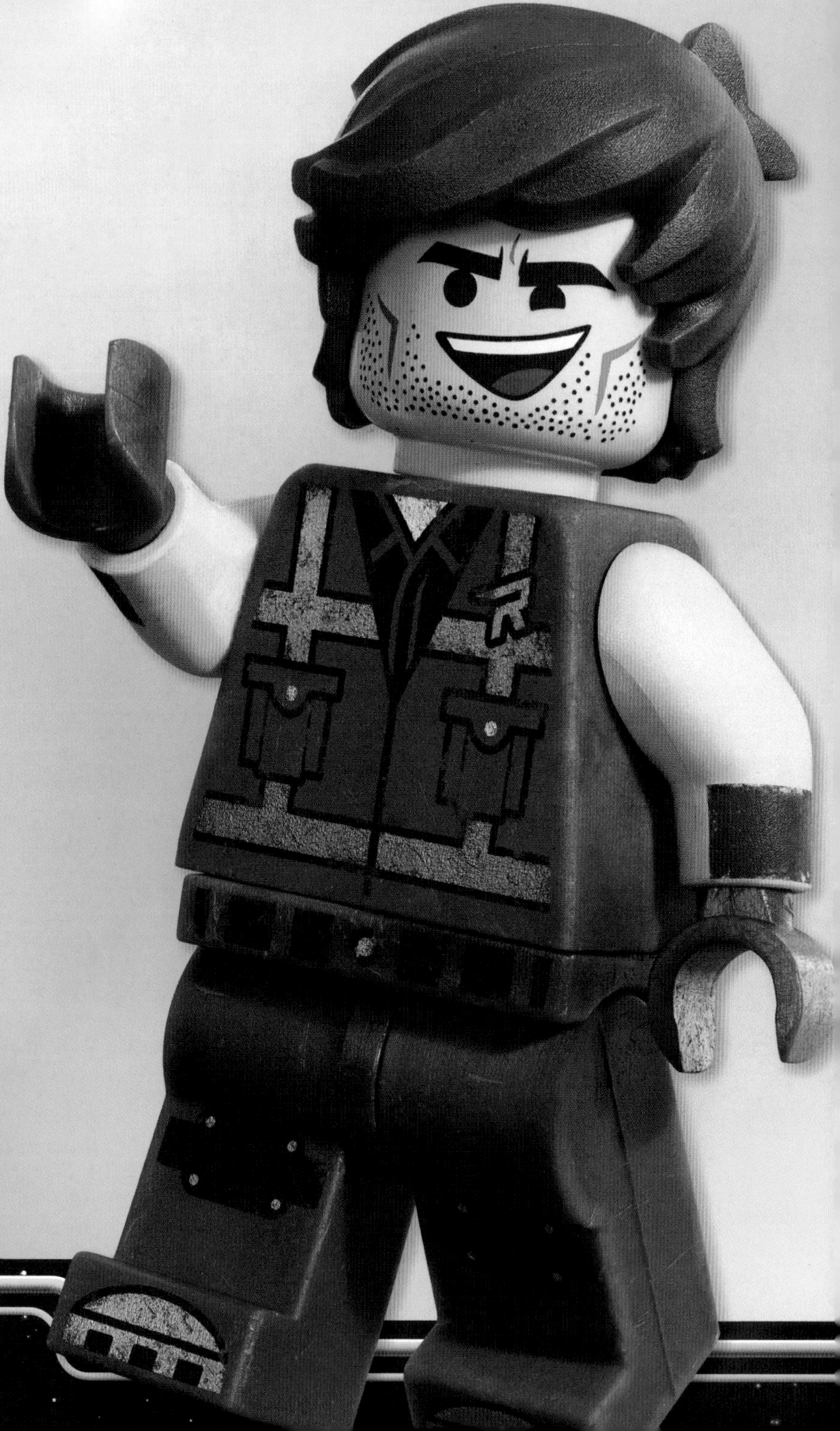

REX DANGERVEST'S TIPS FOR BEING TOUGH

- THERE'S NO GOING BACKWARD IN LIFE. ONLY MOVING FORWARD, AND SOMETIMES STANDING STILL IN A CHILL, RELAXED WAY.

- DON'T WORRY IF YOU DON'T KNOW WHAT YOU'RE DOING. JUST ACT LIKE YOU DO. THAT'S CALLED LEADERSHIP.

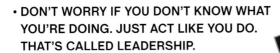

- RAPTORS SHOULD BE RENAMED *RAD*-TORS. YOU KNOW. BECAUSE THEY'RE RAD.

Rextreme

- STUBBLE IS ALWAYS A STRONG CHOICE.

- ANY TIME IS A GOOD TIME TO SPACE SUIT UP.

- STAY WOKE.

BATMAN'S TIPS FOR BEING TOUGH

- BATS ARE TOUGH.

- CITADELS ARE TOUGH.

- HAVING NINE MOVIES MADE ABOUT YOU IS A SUPER-TOUGH LOOK.

- IF YOU REALLY WANT TO BE TOUGH, THEN YOU NEED TO:
    - ☐ DRESS LIKE ME.
    - ☐ WALK LIKE ME.
    - ☐ TALK LIKE ME.
    - ☐ BUT REMEMBER, YOU'RE NOT ME.
    - ☐ BECAUSE I'M BATMAN.

What's your best tip for being tough?

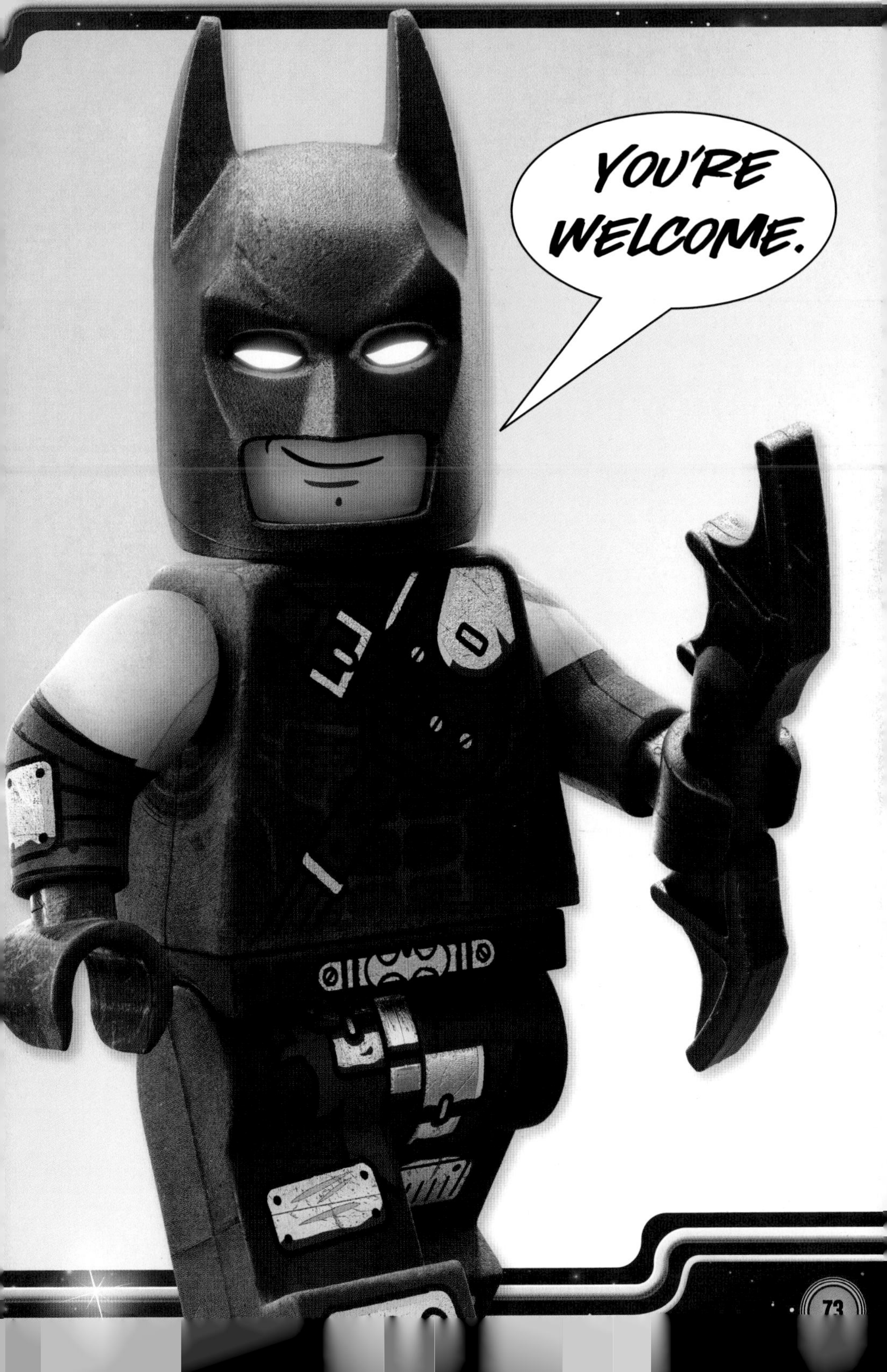
YOU'RE WELCOME.

EMMET'S AWESOME PIECE OF ADVICE #4: SOMETIMES YOU'VE GOT TO BREAK THINGS DOWN TO BUILD THEM BACK UP.

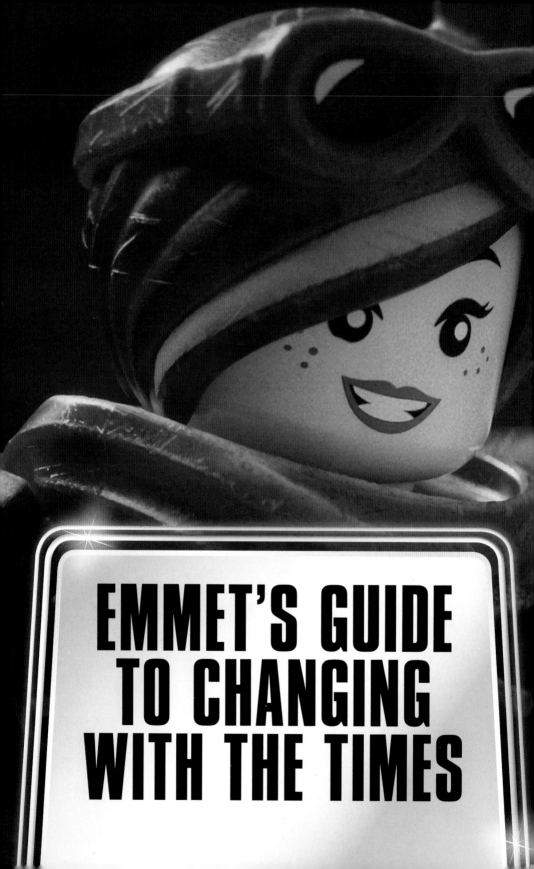

EMMET'S GUIDE TO CHANGING WITH THE TIMES

MAKE IT WORK FOR YOU

If you're going to successfully keep the awesome alive during the whole (second part) of an adventure, it's really, really, *really* important to change with the times. I don't mean big things like changing your entire personality, your outlook on life, or how you take your coffee in the morning. I mean learning to change the things that will help make you a better person. Like being courageous in the face of uncertainty. Or learning to build a spaceship that won't collapse in an asteroid belt. Or summoning the chutzpah to be a leader and do what's right even when you're 100 percent sure you have zero percent clue what you're doing.

People always think, "Oh, look! There's sweet ol' Emmet! He can't change with the times and be rough and tumble when it matters the most." But that's totally not true! I learned to toughen up in order to save my friends, just in a unique way that worked for me. And you can too!

LEARNING TO BUILD HARDCORE VEHICLES

When the aliens started attacking, I had to pull out all the stops on my Master Building skills and come up with some kick-butt vehicles! Check out my best designs.

LIGHTNING-FAST GETAWAY CAR

Lucy and I quick-built this sweet ride to escape alien invaders. Lucy added the super-argo turbo engine, powerful missiles, and spiky blaster cannon. I built the snazzy racing stripes, windshield wipers, and super-safe taillight blinker. I guess you could say my first attempt at changing with the times was a work in progress!

CHANGING
WITH THE TIMES
BEGINNER
SUCCESS!

TRIPLE-DECKER COUCH MECH

When Sweet Mayhem attacked, I came *this* close to stopping her with my Triple-Decker Couch Mech. Okay, well, technically she blasted it apart with one shot of her sticker gun. But I still managed to come up with one of my best battle insults ever because of it: "You're pushin' for a cushion!"

CHANGING WITH THE TIMES KINDA SUCCESS!

HOUSE ROCKET

The thought of my friends being in danger made me realize this wasn't the time for cutesy-wootsy meditation rooms and double-decker porch swings. This was a time for bold design choices, like giving my house rocket thrusters, internal combustion engines, and a cool bridge station like on those late-night sci-fi movies.

CHANGING WITH THE TIMES ACTUAL SUCCESS!

What would your hardcore vehicle look like?

TIPS FOR DEALING WITH NEW FOES

When going on an interstellar rescue mission, you're bound to encounter bizarre aliens you've never seen before. And when that happens, you need to be ready to change your tactics on the fly. Take it from me, it sure would have been great to have a guide like this so I knew what I was getting into. Lucky for you, you DO have this guide. Ooooh! I should totally time travel and read this guide!!

TIP #1:
Don't fall for adorable weapons of fiery destruction. They may look happy, but they're really just trying to explode in your face.

TIP #2:
Seriously, if they come up to you with big puppy-dog eyes and say they love you, they STILL just want to explode in your face.

LOVE YOU MORE!

TIP #3:

Don't try to go up against a sticker gun. If Batman can't beat it, do you really think any of us can?

TIP #4:

If a suspicious shape-shifting queen tries to convince you about how <u>not</u> evil she is, you may want to consider the possibility that she is actually evil.

SURF'S UP!

TIP #5:

Use strange alien features to your advantage, like octo-alien surfing.

TIP #6:

When in doubt, remember that the cuter an alien is, the more likely it wants to eat you.

OM NOM NOM!

I'M NOT SALTY. I'M JUST LAYERED.

TIP #7:

Don't assume that an alien who looks sweet is actually sweet. They could turn out to be a little salty.

TIP #8:

If strange alien forces capture you, bring you to a spa, and offer you an array of relaxation services . . . you may actually want to try it out.

Shambhala Health Spa and Mindfulness Center Treatment Menu

Hot Stone Massage $0

Mirror Glaze Nail Gel $0

Glitter Scrub $0

Sparkle Rinse $0

Rainbow Spray Tan $0

Exfoliating Fondant Wrap $0

Sweet Almond Body Soak $0

Just knowing you're relaxed
is payment enough!

NAMASTE.

DO WHAT IT TAKES

And sometimes, you just have to find it within yourself to do whatever it takes to save the people you love. Even if it means journeying to a whole new universe and being scared out of your mind but forcing yourself to keep going because your friends need you and you can't let them down. After all, if you can't find it within yourself to make the change, then how can anything *be* changed?

**EMMET'S AWESOME PIECE OF ADVICE #5:
YOU DON'T JUST HAVE WHAT IT TAKES.
YOU *ARE* WHAT IT TAKES.**

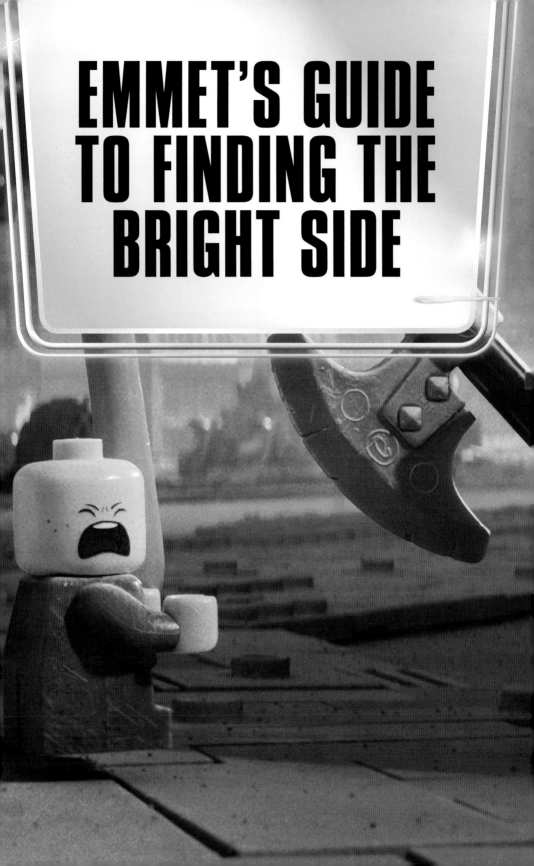

THERE'S ALWAYS A BRIGHT SIDE!

Okay, enough with all the bleakness, and change, and general annihilation. It's time to take a look at the good old bright side. I guarantee you, there are tons of bright, sparkly moments of pure joy in the apocalypse—you just have to know where to find them!

UNEXPECTED BRIGHT SPOTS
(OF THE APOCALYPSE)

Overpriced coffee for two still exists and is double the caffeinated fun!!

Raptors love belly rubs!

Cool-guy handshakes can go on for like, ten minutes while free-falling in outer space. Heck yeah!

Sewer babies are surprisingly cute!

There's always that slight chance an alien spaceship will surprise you with a dance party mode.

GET FUNKY!

DON'T GET TRICKED!

Queen Watevra Wa'nabi *may* have been trying to trick my friends. Here are some things you can do instead of listening to her!

EMMETS TIPS TO AVOIDING BEING GETTING TRICKED BY ALIENS

- COVER YOUR EARS!

- IF YOU HAVE HEADPHONES WITH YOU, USE THEM AS EARPLUGS AND LISTEN TO SOMETHING ELSE.

- TRY TO RESIST THE URGE TO DANCE ALONG. (EVEN IF YOUR FOOT STARTS TAPPING!)

- WHATEVER YOU DO, DONT SING! I SAID DONT . . .

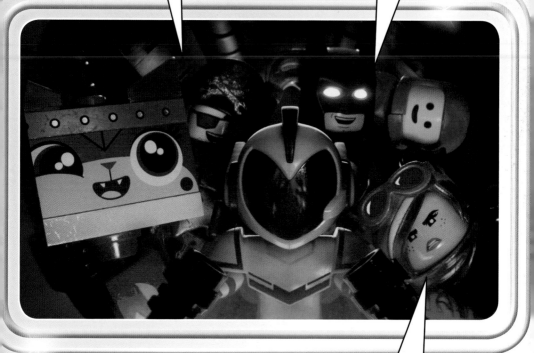

EMMET'S AWESOME PIECE OF ADVICE #6: FRIENDS WHO DANCE TOGETHER, STAY TOGETHER.

EMMET'S GUIDE TO SAVING WHAT MATTERS

FACING THE TRUTH

As hard as it is to admit, I was really afraid of losing the people I cared about most forever because I wasn't tough enough and able to change with the times. But what I learned along the way was that I didn't need to change who I was in order to save what mattered most. I needed to change how I thought about myself and believe that I had what it took to save my friends inside of me all along.

EMMET'S PERSONALITY	WEAKNESS?	OR STRENGTH?
Sweet and caring	Not battle ready	Always willing to give new people a chance
Trusting	Easily taken advantage of by alien invaders	Believes in his friends no matter what
Loves anything double- or triple-deckered	Not the strongest battle vehicles . . .	. . . or are they?
Always happy	Leads to awkward moments	Keeps up team morale
Overly optimistic	Doesn't know when to quit	Never quits

EMBRACING THE PAST

And in the end, I realized that all my experiences and everything that had ever helped shape who I am today were all parts of what would help me save the future.

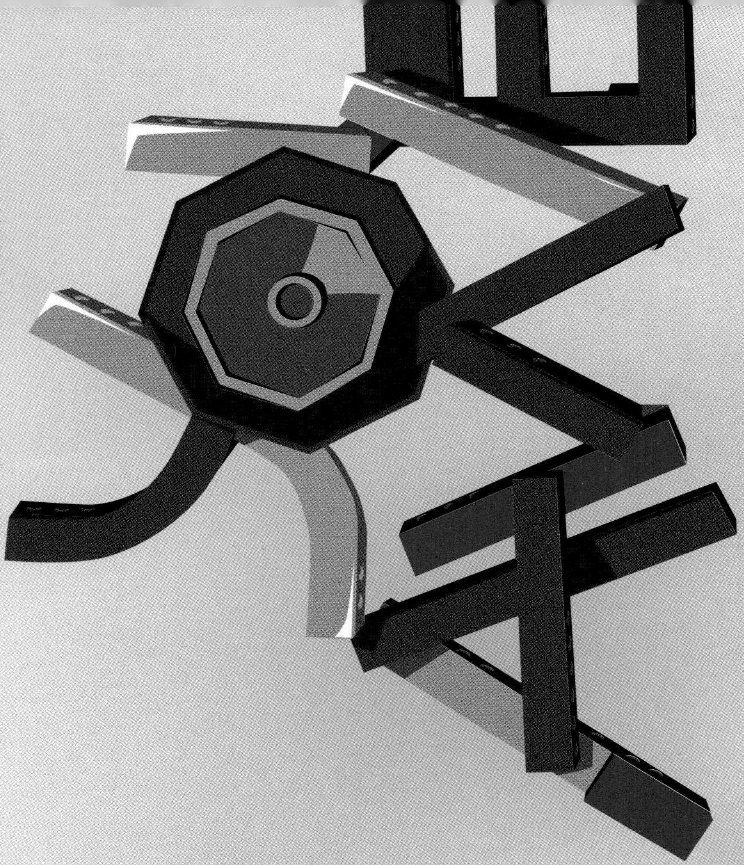

YOUR PAST IS WHAT HELPS YOU BUILD YOUR FUTURE.

QUIZ: YOUR AWESOME PAST

What are things from your past that have made you who you are today? Answer these questions to help you discover what experiences will help you build your future!

1. What is your favorite childhood memory?

2. What are your favorite things to do?

3. What is the accomplishment you're most proud of?

4. What was an experience that made you change your outlook on things?

5. Who are the people that mean the most to you?

6. How do your friends and family help you be the best you can be?

7. Who is someone you admire?

8. What are your dreams and goals?

EMMET'S GUIDE TO REBUILDING THE FUTURE

TOGETHER YOU CAN MAKE IT HAPPEN

Even when new people or new places (or even new alien invaders!) seem super different and weird, part of what makes building the future so awesome is working together to make it happen. Open your ears and your heart. Really listen to what people *not* like you are saying and see if it can make you a better person.

I BELIEVE IN YOU. I'VE SEEN WHO YOU ARE, AND I KNOW WHO YOU CAN BE.

You never know. You might just end up saving the universe. Again.

BUILDING THE FUTURE

What are some ways you would work together to build a brighter future? Try using these ideas for inspiration, and then come up with some of your own!

1. Host a LEGO brick-building party where everyone comes up with one unique design for a building, and then connect them all together to make a super-cool combined town!

2. Write a story about a group of Super Heroes that uses its inner awesome to save the day.

3. Design a cool invention that would help make the world a better place. Then try building a model of it out of LEGO bricks!

4. Start a sharing club where you and your friends meet once a week and each brings a different toy or something cool you want to share so you can all play together.

5. Tell your friends something awesome you admire about them. Then ask them to pay it forward by giving another friend an awesome compliment. Pretty soon, your whole community will be feeling cool together!

THE MORE YOU SHARE YOUR INNER AWESOME, THE MORE AWESOME THE WORLD WILL BE!

EMMET'S AWESOME PIECE OF ADVICE #8: EVERYTHING IS AS AWESOME AS YOU MAKE IT.

GOOD-BYE

KEEP THAT AWESOME ALIVE

Well all right—we did it! We kept the awesome going in spite of insurmountable odds and even in the face of the apocalypse. And I gotta say, I feel pretty great! I hope you do too. Not everyone can keep the groove going when it's the end of the world, but you picked up this book, dove right in, and said, "Heck yeah, Emmet—we're not just going to keep things awesome, we're going to make it awesomer!" I can't wait to do it again. And I'm sure we will. I know this is the end of the second part of the adventure. But like Batman says, there are always more adventures in various stages of development. I'm not sure exactly what that means, but if I had to guess, it means we'll be seeing each other again to keep the awesomefest going. Probably sooner than you think. Catch you on the flip!

THE END